MEOW!

VICTORIA YING

HARPER

An Imprint of HarperCollinsPublishers

ISBN 978-0-06-244096-9 (trade bdg.)
The artist used Adobe Photoshop® to create the digital illustrations for this book.
17 18 19 20 21 SCP 10 9 8 7 6 5 4 3 2 1
❖
First Edition

For everyone who has ever loved a fluffy, noisy hairball

meow...?

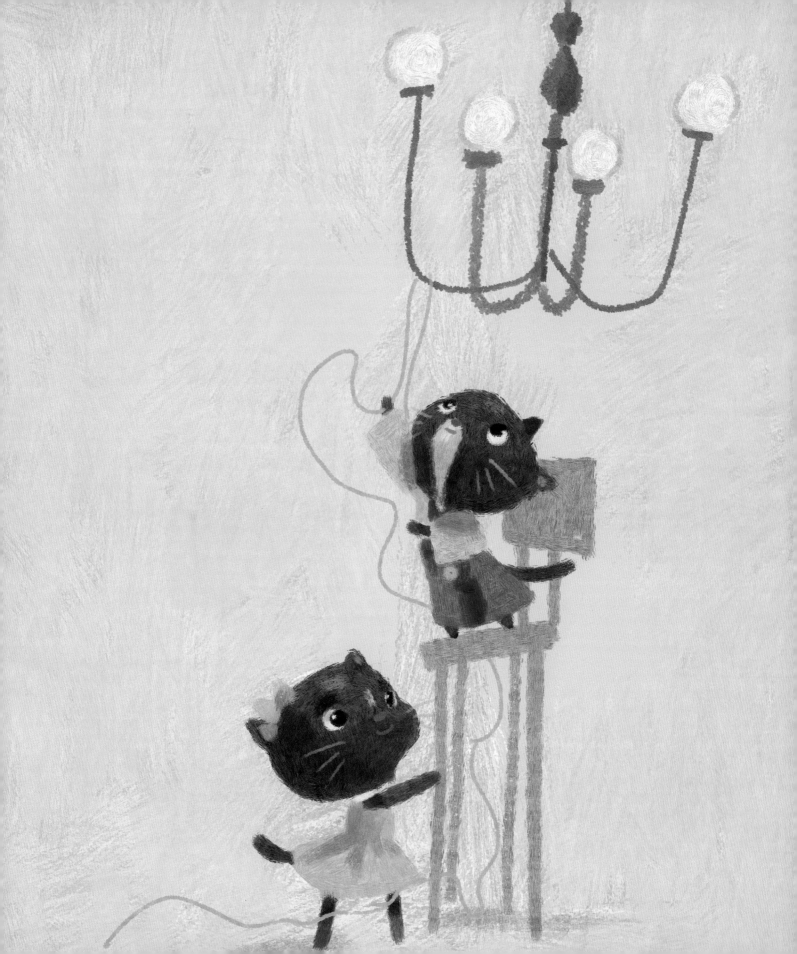